Milly had a bug-nut. She won it at a party. The bug-nut was a little wooden box in the shape of a walnut. Inside there was an insect with white wings suspended on a pin. When Milly opened the box, the wings wobbled and made the insect look alive.

Milly's bug-nut was very hard to open, so hard that Milly thought that it would be the perfect place to put her secret, most precious wish. So this is where she put it.

Milly had wonderful long, dark curly hair.
Mum's friends would say, "I've just spent loads of
money at the hairdressers trying to make my hair
look like that!" And then they would laugh at
their little joke and make Milly feel uncomfortable.

Milly had dark eyes too, as dark as the sky
when the stars come out.

She was pretty and gentle and sensible and
funny and everybody liked her but if you looked
very hard, you might think that underneath she

Milly's Bug-Nut

Jill Janney

For Jemima and Matthew
and for all children who have lost someone they love.
J.J.

First published in the United Kingdom in 2002 by Winston's Wish
This edition ©2002 Winston's Wish
Text copyright ©2002 Jill Janney
Illustrations copyright ©2002 Peter Bailey
ISBN 978-0-9539123-4-6
A CIP catalogue record for this book is available from the British Library.

Editorial consultant, Jane Fior, The Cancer Counselling Trust
Designed by Vicky Fullick

Milly's Bug-Nut

Jill Janney

Illustrated by Peter Bailey

Winston's Wish

was a little bit sad, even though she didn't say so.
Milly had a younger brother, Ben. He was cheeky
and brave and incredibly good at football and
sums. He would announce the football scores as
soon as he was picked up from school and he
was always adding tens and units in his head.
He didn't look a little bit sad in the way that
Milly did, but sometimes he got cross. In fact,
sometimes he got very cross, really angry, and
punched things including Milly and Mum.

Milly and Ben's mum went to work three days a week and she was always stressed out. Sometimes she was fun and then she would dance with Milly and Ben in the sitting room, or take them riding over the go-slow bumps in the road, or talk their secret language.

"Oshi badlet-up nostro padlop?"

"Mashi moffi kaka," Milly would giggle in reply.

Sometimes Mum gave them the biggest hugs imaginable and listened to everything they said but every now and then, especially when Milly and Ben made a mess or wouldn't go to bed, she exploded! Afterwards she would say sorry and talk about 'coping' and how difficult it all was.

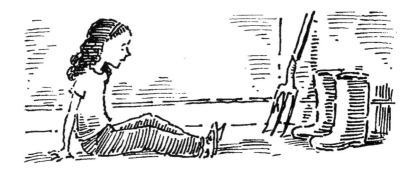

Milly and Ben's Dad wasn't there any more. Ben said he was all around them, especially in the car, but Milly didn't know where he was. More than anything else in the world, she wanted to see him again.

Milly remembered the morning when Mum told them that the doctors hadn't been able to make Dad better. She told them that Dad had died. Ben had laughed and thought that Mum was joking but Milly knew at once what it meant and felt a huge sadness that started in her tummy, spread up through her heart (which Milly knew was on the left-hand side) and up into her face, where it squeezed two big tears from her dark eyes.

Milly was young then. When you are young, it's not very easy to understand what happens when someone dies. Mum told Milly that it's not easy when you're a grown-up either.

They lit a candle.

They sent balloons into the sky for Dad.

They talked about him.

They cried. Mum cried the most. Milly and Ben would stand by her, feeling sad and wanting her to stop.

That was when Milly put her secret, most precious wish into the bug-nut.

Grandma and Grandpa came to stay but Mum sent them home after a few days. Some people gave Milly and Ben presents and at school, the Christmas carol concert collection was given to help doctors find ways to cure her Daddy's illness which made Milly feel special.

Mum said that right now they were probably feeling,

sad, sad, sad, *happy*
sad, sad, sad, *happy*

but as time went on they would feel,

happy, happy, happy, sad,
happy, happy, happy, sad.

Milly liked this and always remembered to tell Mum when she was feeling happy because she thought this would cheer Mum up.

Milly made an ordinary drawer in her bedside cupboard become special. She put a photograph of Dad in it, hugging her tightly on a hill top. Milly's curly dark hair and Dad's curly dark hair mingled together in the wind. Dad's eyes were bursting with pride and Milly's were full of happiness and excitement.

Sometimes Mum would ask if she could open the drawer and look at the photograph.

Then she would say to Milly,

"Did your Dad love you? What do you think?"

And Milly would laugh, feeling a warm glow in her heart when she thought of Dad. Although they didn't always agree on everything, especially when it was the right time to go to bed, she always knew he loved her.

In the drawer, next to the photograph, she placed a wooden doll that Mum had said was from Dad, the Christmas after he died, and a book that had a picture of a man that reminded Milly of her Dad.

Milly didn't look in the drawer every day but she thought of it as Dad's drawer and that was a nice thought.

Milly put her bug-nut on top of the bedside
cupboard. Because it was so special, she
wanted to keep it safe, somewhere where she
could see it. Every night, before she went to
sleep, she would hold it in her hand and think
of her secret, most precious wish and hope that
it would come true soon.

Ben said he wanted a dad. All the other children had dads. It wasn't fair. He didn't like it when Mum kicked the ball when it landed at her feet at football practice on Saturday morning. That's what dads did, not mums.

Sometimes when he was feeling tired or cross, he would kick the door and say, "Why can't my Dad just be here?" and sometimes when Mum and Milly were feeling sad, he would try and feel sad too. Sometimes he could say he missed him but often he couldn't.

Sometimes he would take Milly's bug-nut and hide it but he never tried to open it because Milly had said that if he did, a huge monster would appear from under the house and eat him up, and Ben believed her. And he always put it back before bedtime.

There were times at school when Milly felt sad, particularly if someone had been unkind to her. When this happened, Milly would remember her bug-nut and the photograph in her special drawer and she would think of her Dad and feel as if, somehow, he could protect her from all danger.

She told Mrs Robinson, her teacher. Mrs Robinson thought that Milly was special and Milly thought she was special too, and somehow knew how she felt. Milly explained to Mrs Robinson that her heart beat in a different way since Dad had died and that she always felt something was missing. She didn't say this to Mum in case it upset her.

On Dad's special day, Mum took them out of school. On the first anniversary they went to the tree where Mum had scattered Dad's ashes. Milly knew that Dad had been cremated. This meant that his body had been burnt as it wasn't needed any more and that the ashes were what was left.

You could see the tree from the top of the hill and Milly ran as fast as she could to get there.

Her feet squelched in the mud and the cold wind stung her ears but the old oak's branches reached down to the ground just as if Dad was holding out his arms to catch her and lift her up into the sky.

On the second anniversary they went to Disneyland Paris. On the way back Milly insisted on going to the top of the Eiffel Tower. She bought a black purse for her best friend Connie and a glass for Mrs Robinson. Ben bought a headband with MICKEY on it.

It was hard to think of Dad when they were having so much fun but Mum looked sad and that upset Milly. That night she held her bug-nut tight and made her special wish.

Milly knew when Mum was sad. Milly knew this even though other people didn't. Mum would smile and laugh, go to work, pick them up from school, cook and take care of the house and look nice when she went out.

But Milly knew that she was still sad.

A man called Paul appeared. Paul's wife had died. Paul had two boys. At first, Mum smiled a lot when Paul was around and this made Milly happy. Milly didn't mind when Mum kissed him or gave him a hug and was quite happy to climb onto Paul's lap and get a hug as well. Ben loved playing with the two boys and Milly joined in as best she could to please Mum but she didn't like it when Mum tried to talk to her about Paul.

"Do you like him, Milly? What about the boys? Do you like spending time with them? Oh, I don't know, I'm so confused."

Milly tried to be helpful but she didn't know what to say. She was glad when Mum changed the subject and gave her a hug.

Milly still heard Mum crying sometimes, after she and Ben had gone to bed, and after a while they stopped seeing Paul and the boys.

"I think it's for the best," Mum said.

"You don't mind, do you?"

Milly didn't mind. Milly was far too busy to mind about Paul. She had Connie, Alice and Lucy to think about. They were a gang. They had to agree a password and decide which games to play. You could only play if you were in the gang. They let Ben join in if he agreed to be the dog which he always did because he liked crawling around on all fours, making silly barking noises and falling over.

Milly was busy thinking about things she wanted and sometimes got, like Game Boys and Play Stations, videos and computer games, and bendy pencils that you could tie into knots and buy for £1.99 at the little shop on the corner.

And Milly was busy at school, learning her times tables and spelling and how the Egyptians used to wrap up their dead and bury them in a box with an eye painted on it so that the dead person could see out.

They used to surround them with cooking things too. This was because the Egyptians believed that when you died, you went on to another life and so needed everyday things. Milly didn't think that this was true, but if it was, she wondered how her Daddy was managing without his tool kit because he'd always loved doing jobs around the house. She didn't like to ask the teacher and she didn't ask Mum either.

Milly was busy with other things too. There were trips to the cinema, weekends in country cottages, pizzas, parties and sleep-overs, birthdays and Christmas. There was dancing on Monday, judo on Tuesday and recorder on Thursday. And of course, she had Poppy her rabbit and Buster her hamster to look after.

Although Milly was so busy, she still thought about Dad, and sometimes she looked at the photograph in the drawer, and sometimes she held her bug-nut for a moment before she went to sleep but often she had had such a busy day that she fell fast asleep straight after Mum's goodnight kiss.

O n the evening of Milly's ninth birthday,
something happened.

Milly was in bed or rather on it because it
was very hot. She was feeling sleepy and the
book that Mum had given her as a present
slipped out of her hands and knocked against
her bedside table. The bug-nut fell to the floor.
It cracked open.

Milly jumped out of bed. Her secret, most
precious wish was out! She ran around the
room, catching flickers of evening sun that
filtered through her half-drawn curtains. Her
heart thumped. Maybe the secret, most precious
wish was about to come true.

When Dad died, Milly had been told that
dead people don't come back, at least not in the
way that you want them to, not in a way that
lets you touch them and hear them and see
them for real. Milly couldn't believe that she
would never see her Dad again and this was the
wish that she had hidden in the bug-nut, to see
him just once more.

Milly looked out into the night. Everything
looked so beautiful. The clouds were edged

with a golden light and in the garden, Milly
could see that her favourite flower, the evening
primrose, had just opened. Suddenly a little wind
blew across the garden and made the leaves on
the trees shiver.

Milly waited. She waited some more. She took
a long, deep breath, the sort of breath that you
have to take when you go to the doctor with a
very bad cough and he listens to your chest
with a stethoscope.

Then something very surprising happened. Milly's toes and fingers began to tingle and her heart felt warmer than it ever had before. Suddenly, quite clearly, Milly knew exactly where her Dad was. He was in her heart and he was there for always.

Milly got back into bed. She could hear Mum downstairs in the kitchen, and in the bedroom next to her own, Ben was counting to a hundred in a silly voice. Milly smiled. She thought now I am,

happy, happy, happy, sad,
happy, happy, happy, sad.

Milly looked at the broken bug-nut on the floor. She didn't think she'd need it any more so she leaned out of bed and picked it up and wondered what to do with it.

She stroked the wings of the little insect and then she put the two halves of the nut box together so that it looked closed and not broken.

She squeezed it in her hand and then she opened Dad's special drawer and placed the bug-nut carefully on the book beside the wooden doll, just in front of the photograph.

She closed the drawer.

Ben had got to sixty-seven by the time darkness gathered across the summer evening sky but by then, Milly was fast asleep.

A Note From the Author

When my husband died, my immediate concerns were for my children. How would they cope? Would they feel comfortable talking about him? What did they understand about death? How would they feel, seeing me upset?

I was aware that talking plainly about death and loss can be difficult for young children, so I searched for a children's book that dealt with the death of a parent, a story book that we could read together and use to share our feelings. However, my search found only books dealing with the death of a pet or a grandparent. So I decided to write my own story, our story, but changing the names of the children and a few little details so that they could identify with it, yet think it was about someone else.

As I began writing *Milly's Bug-Nut*, I would read passages to my children and they would add little bits. My daughter, Mima, described how she felt as if her heart beat in a different way since her Dad died and my son Matthew said how sometimes he found it hard to cry when he really wanted to. I added both these and other comments to the story so it became a wonderful way of sharing and expressing our feelings together.

Later, we watched a documentary on television about Winston's Wish and saw how Winston's Wish encourage the sharing and expressing of feelings as part of the healing process. We knew immediately that we wanted to share *Milly's Bug-Nut* with other families.

Looking back, there are, of course, times when I wish my children had their Dad to guide them and add another dimension to their lives. However, I believe that because we talked, because we shared our feelings together, the children have not only come to terms with their loss but also have a sure sense of who their Dad was and how much he loved them; they can take this with them throughout their lives.

JILL JANNEY

Other titles and products available from Winston's Wish

MEMORY BOXES

A wonderful range of memory boxes for the safekeeping of significant things connected with the person who has died.

A CHILD'S GRIEF

Supporting a child when someone in their family has died
ISBN 978-0-9539123-6-0

AS BIG AS IT GETS

Supporting a child when someone in their family is seriously ill
ISBN 978-0-9539123-2-2

THE SECRET C

Straight Talking About Cancer
ISBN 978-0-9539123-0-8

Winston's Wish
Helpline: 08452 03 04 05

The Winston's Wish Helpline is a national helpline offering support, information and guidance to all those caring for a child or young person who has been bereaved.

Web: www.winstonswish.org.uk

Our website contains a wealth of information for parents and professionals, including schools. The emphasis throughout is on providing easy access to practical, straightforward information, guidance and support.

Email: info@winstonswish.org.uk

MILLY KNOWS THAT WHEN PEOPLE DIE THEY can't come back, not in the way we want them to. But this doesn't stop Milly wishing a secret and very important wish.

MILLY'S BUG-NUT is the story of a family finding their way through bereavement and of Milly who finds an unexpected answer to her heart's desire.

The award-winning charity *Winston's Wish* specialises in supporting families through the many challenges presented by serious illness and death.

Jill Janney, author of MILLY'S BUG-NUT, wrote this story for her own children after the death of their father.

ISBN 978-0-9539123-4-6

Winston's Wish
the charity for bereaved children

Winston's Wish is a Registered Charity
(England and Wales) 1061359, (Scotland) SCO41140

www.winstonswish.org.uk